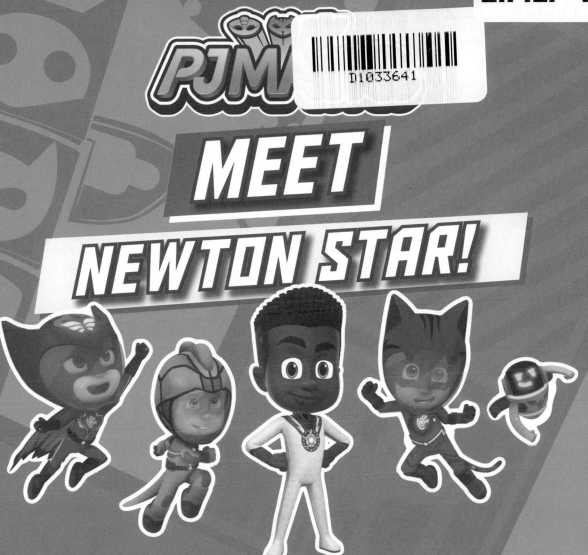

PJM MEET NEWTON STAR!

Based on the episodes "Asteroid Accident" and "All About Asteroids"

Simon Spotlight

New York London Toronto Sydney New Delhi

SIMON SPOTLIGHT
An imprint of Simon & Schuster Children's Publishing Division
1230 Avenue of the Americas, New York, New York 10020
This Simon Spotlight edition August 2021
This book is based on the TV series PJ MASKS © Frog Box/Entertainment One UK Limited. Les Pyjamasques by Romuald © 2007 Gallimard Jeunesse.
This book © 2021 Entertainment One UK Limited. All Rights Reserved. HASBRO and all related logos and trademarks TM & © 2021 Hasbro.
Adapted by Maggie Testa from the series PJ Masks.
All rights reserved, including the right of reproduction in whole or in part in any form.
SIMON SPOTLIGHT and colophon are registered trademarks of Simon & Schuster, Inc.
For information about special discounts for bulk purchases, please contact Simon & Schuster Special Sales at 1-866-506-1949 or business@simonandschuster.com.
Manufactured in the United States of America 0721 LAK
2 4 6 8 10 9 7 5 3 1
ISBN 978-1-5344-9505-0 (pbk)
ISBN 978-1-5344-9506-7 (ebook)

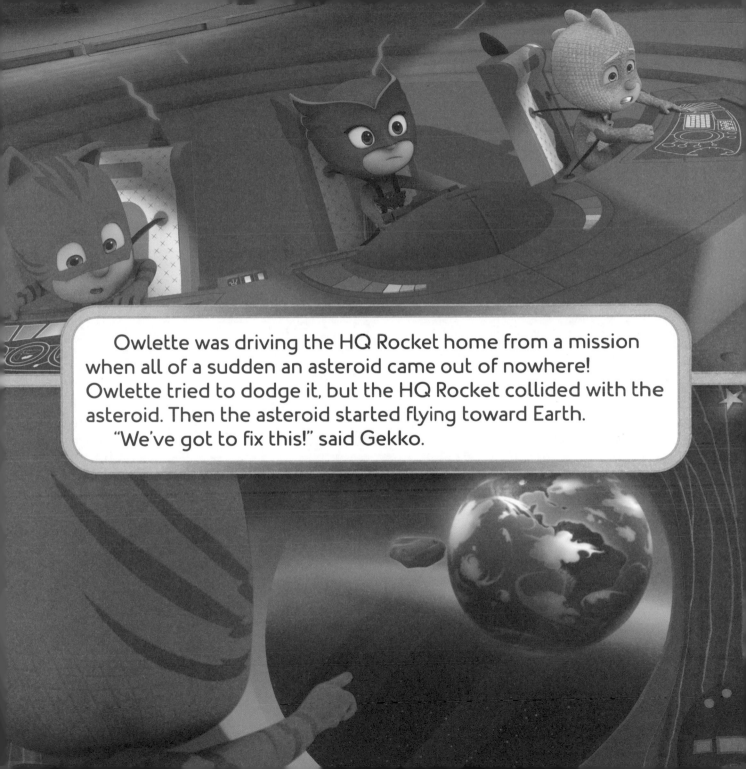

Owlette was driving the HQ Rocket home from a mission when all of a sudden an asteroid came out of nowhere! Owlette tried to dodge it, but the HQ Rocket collided with the asteroid. Then the asteroid started flying toward Earth.

"We've got to fix this!" said Gekko.

The asteroid landed on Earth—right in front of Romeo!

Romeo couldn't believe his good luck. "An asteroid? Fallen out of the sky, just for me?"

But before he could run off with it, the PJ Masks landed the HQ Rocket and started running toward the asteroid.

Romeo would have to come back for it the next night. The PJ Masks would be ready for him.

Amaya was upset about the asteroid accident.

"It could have landed on the school, the library—anything," she said.

"Don't feel bad, Amaya," Connor reassured her. "We have to take it back into space and send it far, far away."

Connor, Amaya, and Greg went to the library to find books about space. But all the books about space were gone! A boy they had never met was reading all of them! Before they could ask him any questions, he disappeared.

That night, Amaya, Connor, and Greg transformed into Owlette, Catboy, and Gekko. With PJ Robot's help, they came up with a plan to use the HQ Rocket's landing claws to grab the asteroid and take it back into space . . . before Romeo could get his hands on it!

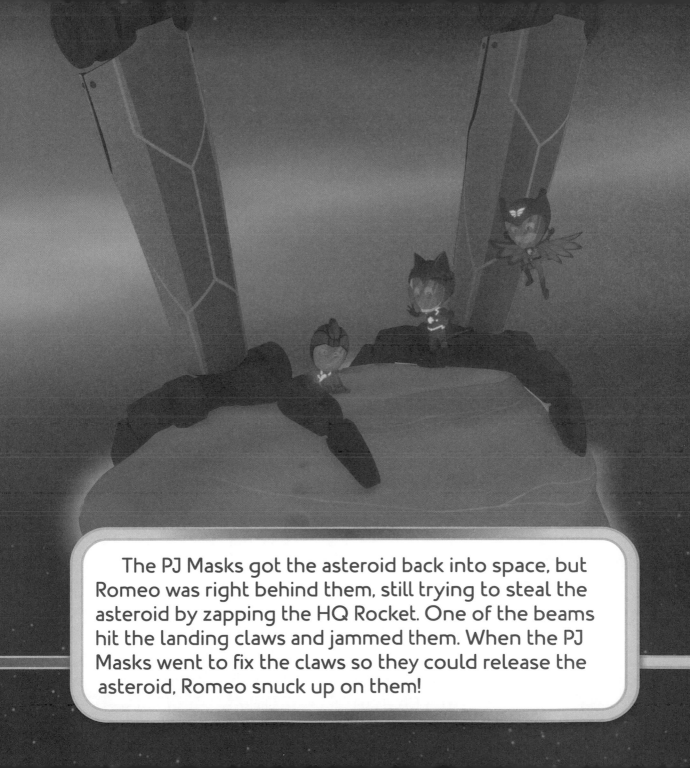

The PJ Masks got the asteroid back into space, but Romeo was right behind them, still trying to steal the asteroid by zapping the HQ Rocket. One of the beams hit the landing claws and jammed them. When the PJ Masks went to fix the claws so they could release the asteroid, Romeo snuck up on them!

Catboy used his Super Cat Stripes, but they backfired. Romeo trapped the PJ Masks on the asteroid! They didn't know what to do next. Suddenly, the boy Owlette had seen in the library was standing on the asteroid!

"Who are you?" asked Catboy.

"I'm Newton," replied the boy. "But at night I'm Newton Star!"

"I saw you in the library," said Owlette.

"Yeah, I go there a lot," replied Newton. "I was trying to work out what to do about this asteroid that I knocked to Earth last night."

"You knocked it?" asked Owlette. "It wasn't me?"

"I was investigating the asteroid, but I rolled it into your spaceship by mistake," explained Newton. "That's why I ran away earlier. I thought you'd be mad."

"Wait. You're a daytime kid?" asked Gekko. "With nighttime powers? A hero?"

"I'm more of a scientist," said Newton. "I come up here and explore the secrets of the universe. I kind of keep to myself."

Newton Star used his powers to free the PJ Masks, and then he began to move the asteroid away from Romeo.

"You're surfing it?" asked Owlette.

"I'm trying," said Newton. "It's one of my powers, but this one's hard. Especially when that kid is zapping it."

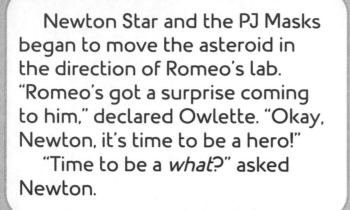

Newton Star and the PJ Masks began to move the asteroid in the direction of Romeo's lab. "Romeo's got a surprise coming to him," declared Owlette. "Okay, Newton, it's time to be a hero!"

"Time to be a *what*?" asked Newton.

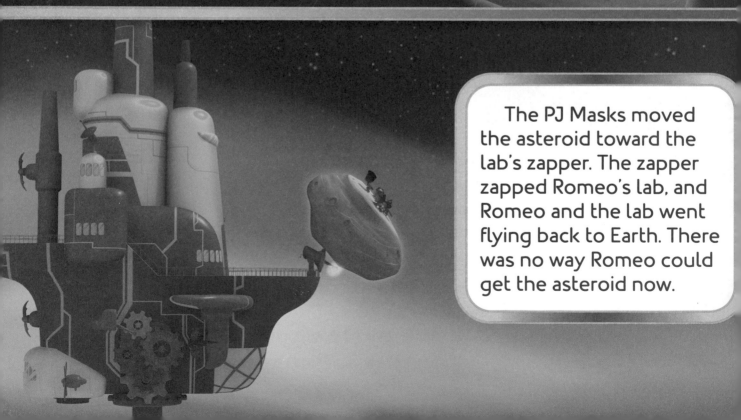

The PJ Masks moved the asteroid toward the lab's zapper. The zapper zapped Romeo's lab, and Romeo and the lab went flying back to Earth. There was no way Romeo could get the asteroid now.

Then Newton Star used his powers to send the asteroid deep into space. He also zoomed the PJ Masks back to the HQ Rocket. The PJ Masks all shouted hooray, because tonight they had met a new nighttime asteroid-surfing friend!

A few nights later, Newton Star was studying asteroids again.

"Ahh, nothing like a bit of space," he said as he moved the asteroids around with his powers.

But little did he know that he had a secret audience watching from the moon: Luna Girl and her little sister, Motsuki!

"Space boy!" said Motsuki.

"Who is he?" wondered Luna Girl. "He's hanging around my moon, doing glowy stuff and getting power."

"Power?" asked Motsuki.

"Are you thinking what I'm thinking?" Luna Girl asked her sister as they made a plan for the next night.

The next day at the library, Amaya, Connor, and Greg caught up to Newton. They had so many questions for him!

"Wasn't that awesome the other night?" asked Greg.

"Are you coming out with us again? Tonight, maybe? Are you?" asked Connor.

"I don't know," answered Newton.

"At least let us come and see your space powers. They're awesome!" said Amaya.

"There's nothing to see, really," said Newton. "I'm still experimenting."

"I love experiments!" said Amaya. "Can we watch? Please?"

"I guess," replied Newton.

Amaya cheered. "We're going to find out about space power!"

That night, the PJ Masks met up with Newton Star in space. They had a lot of questions. Newton was starting to get overwhelmed. So he sent the PJ Masks on a little ride around the moon so he could focus on his experiment.

But as soon as the PJ Masks were out of sight, Luna Girl and Motsuki put their plan into action.

"Who are you?" Newton asked when Motsuki appeared next to him.

"Eeep!" Motsuki replied. Luna Girl trapped Newton Star in a bubble from her Luna Wand. She brought him to the moon, where she planned to drain his power for her Mega Magnet.

Newton was trapped, but he knew there were three people not too far away who could help him. He sent a signal out to the PJ Masks.

It wasn't long before the PJ Masks saw
Newton Star's signal. They followed the path of
green asteroids back to Newton, but Luna Girl
had set a trap.

The PJ Masks were now trapped in the Luna Fortress with Newton Star. Luna Girl would drain *all* their powers!

"This is my fault," Newton Star confessed. "I sent you away to get some peace, but then I brought you into this."

"You sent us away?" Owlette asked.

"I'm sorry," Newton replied. "I like space and quiet when I work. But I shouldn't have pushed you away."

"It's our fault too," said Owlette. "We were trying too hard to be your friend. It's okay if you need some space."

"Friends come in handy, like when villains are around," said Gekko.

"Yeah, that figures," said Newton.

"Now we need to figure our way out," added Catboy.

Luckily, Newton had an idea. They could run up the walls of the fortress and surprise Luna Girl and Motsuki.

Then they could use the asteroids that Newton had powered to pop Luna Girl's bubbles.

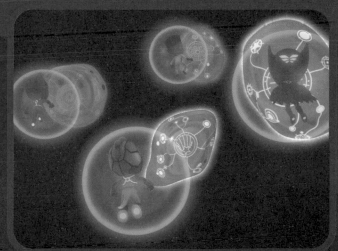

Soon they were free from the bubbles.
"Star shields!" said Newton as Luna Girl and Motsuki tried to blast at them.
"You have shields too? Awesome!" exclaimed Gekko.

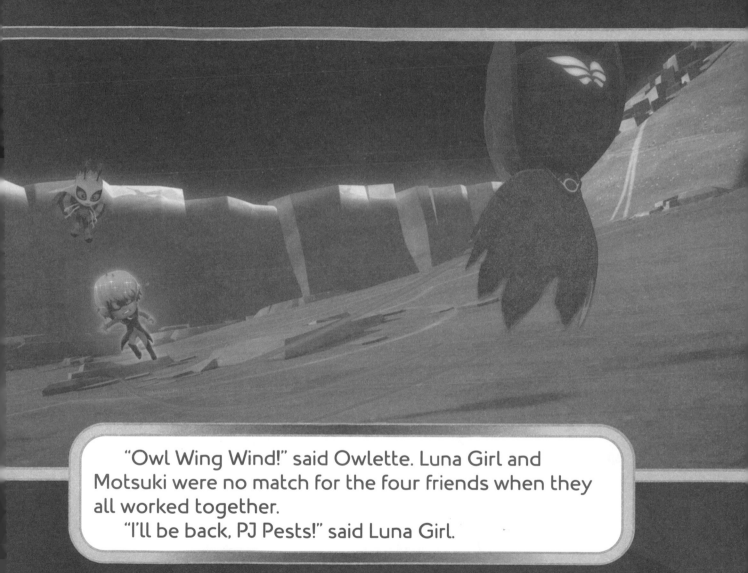

"Owl Wing Wind!" said Owlette. Luna Girl and Motsuki were no match for the four friends when they all worked together.

"I'll be back, PJ Pests!" said Luna Girl.

"Thanks, Newton!" said Catboy.

"We did it!" said Newton.

PJ Robot ran up to Newton Star and began to talk excitedly.

"Shh, PJ Robot," said Catboy. "Newton needs space."

"I need friends, too," said Newton.

PJ Masks all shout hooray, 'cause in the night we saved the day!